Deliver Us from the Evil One

Deliver Us from the Evil One

Matthew 6:13
NIV

Denise C. McCreary

Library of Congress Control Number:		2015911066
ISBN:	Softcover	978-1-5035-8491-4
	eBook	978-1-5035-8490-7

Print information available on the last page.

Rev. date: 08/10/2015

To order additional copies of this book, contact:
Xlibris
1-888-795-4274
www.Xlibris.com
Orders@Xlibris.com
712333

ACKNOWLEDGEMENTS

Lord, I thank you first and foremost because, I couldn't of made it without you, your protection and your love for me when I didn't love myself and for you keeping me when I didn't want to be kept. Lord I thank you.

Mom and dad thank you for visiting me in the County every week for one day and only for an hour riding the Greyhound bus from New York to Virginia, and for all those every weekend visits, putting money in my commissary, so I didn't go without. Mommy taking care of my girls and grand babies , I know it wasn't easy and you cried a lot and there where days you didn't see no way. But God..I love you mommy Thank you, Love you.

My daughter Brittney, my back bone my silent strength, I'm so very proud of the women you became now and while I was away, not a minute went by that my heart did not long to be near you, I was so afraid when I left you, but God. We made it through together. Brittney thank you for bringing my grandson Nazir to see me when he was only two weeks old and every weekend after that for 3 1/2 years.

My daughter Tamina my prayer warrior, when I left Amina was two, it felt like someone ripped my heart out I was so afraid to have to leave you two alone, I would pray that while Amina was sleep that God would kiss her for me and always have our hearts connected, so she could always feel my love for her and I her, and you know what he did because every time she came to visit me it was as if I ever left. Thank you for letting Mommy and Britt bring her to visit me and for all her school work and pictures you sent me .. We made it.... But for the grace of God....

My husband James, I thank God for you, I know it wasn't easy with the girls, but you hung in there with them, some days I know you walked in a daze, every time I asked you what was wrong, you said nothing babe. Thank you for being my best friend , my right hand ... We made it ....Mr. Johnny and Ms. Louise...Thank you .My brother Joe, thank you for paying my restitution so I stayed out of D-dorm... Thank you

Ronald Sellers... Thank you RIP Kenny

I would like to thank Vernon Oliver, Dennis Parker and James Hargrove of Hope Inc, no matter what was said about me , put in the papers and on the news, no matter how bad it got are how emotional distraught I became you guys made sure I was OK. Thank you. Chandra Goodman and Renee Tillery .. Thank you for being there and visiting me I love you guys and Chante Jordan and T. Westmoreland ..Thank you for being there..

THANK YOU

Part One

"'Our Father in heaven, hallowed be your name,
[10] your kingdom come, your will be done, on earth as it is in heaven.
[11] Give us today our daily bread.
[12] And forgive us our debts as we also have forgiven our debtors.
[13] And lead us not into temptation,[1] but deliver us from the evil one.
Matthew 6:9-13, New International Version (NIV)

1

CHAPTER ONE

THE BEGINNING

Reverend Jonathan was a true man of God one who worshiped the Lord and obeyed all God's commandments and stood steadfast on God's moral laws. The reverend wasa man of vision who could see into the past, present and future but lately what he was envisioning about the future, had him in complete despair a feeling he could not ignore.

CHAPTER TWO

The Reverend stood on the banks of the River Forgiveness, which surrounded the land that the Lord had given to his father's so many years ago. He had brought them out of bondage to this great and marvelous land of plenty. The river began to rise, the wind blew fiercely and the sky turned bloody red. There was huge balls of hail crying down upon the earth in despair, for what was to come.

CHAPTER THREE

The reverend stood utterly still staring at what could only be a revelation. A revelation that would certainly be a magnitude's of sin, sin so great that the Evil One would walk the earth killing, stealing and destroying all innocence. There would be wide spread incest, sexual immorality and drunkenness running rampart in this, the land of plenty. What he saw was a land covered in thick black smoke, hails of blood, worldwide screaming and moaning of the innocent souls that were being debauched by evil.

CHAPTER FOUR

The thick black smoke took his breath as he fell upon the ground grasping for air. As he lay on the ground, a black bird, one he never seen before landed in front of him saying "Man of God on this Sunday one hundred and twenty souls will be baptized and cleansed in this the River of Forgiveness. These souls will indeed repent of all their sins and be made whole by the blood of Jesus. Man of God these one hundred and twenty souls that were cleansed and repented of their sins will be the first souls the Evil One will kill, steal and destroy, because of the wickedness of your sins too come."

CHAPTER FIVE

The reverend cried out loud unto the Lord falling prostrate to the ground and the black bird disappeared as suddenly as it had appeared. The ministers and deacons saw him as he slid unto the ground, running towards him to see what was happening they called out the name of Jesus. The women and children looked on as well praying aloud for all to be well with the reverend.

Once the men got closer they could see that he had one of his spells and he was going to be ok; however; this spell had been different than the others and as they helped him upon his feet the reverend whispered "He will not put more on me than I can bear."

CHAPTER SIX

On that Sunday as the blackbird had spoken 120 Souls were baptized in the River of Forgiveness, and, repented of their sins. The spirit was high in the church that day as the church praised God. The reverend sat and looked over his congregation fearing the worst to come, "Lord have mercy on us your children." He whispered.

CHAPTER SEVEN

The years that followed slipped by and the 5th year of their marriage the reverend and his wife had a son a beautiful boy named after his father. Jonathan Jr. would be the next reverend of the Church of Forgiveness just as his father and his father father before.

Jon Jr. was a child of grace and anything he did was done gracefully. His voice whether he was speaking or singing mesmerized and captured the attention of all who was in his presence. By the time Jon was of age his father had instilled in him the prophecy of what was to come if they did not follow God's moral laws.

CHAPTER EIGHT

Jon Jr. a man of vision as his father had a sense of discernment that was astounding. He knew deep in his heart that his father was not telling him everything, well, actually not telling him the entire truth of what was to come. He felt deep within that the key piece to his future depended on what his father would or would not do.

CHAPTER NINE

Jon got home early on that evening only to find his mother crying, his father standing in front of her tears in his eye's. Jon Jr. knew something great was getting ready to happen and it wasn't for the good. "What's happen?" Jon asked his father walking towards his mom. The sky turned Blood red and the trees began to fall with each lighting strike against them one by one like dominos. "what's happening dad?" Jon Jr. yelled making his way to his mother, "Jr." his father said as he helped his father pull his mother out the chair and ran towards the church for safety.

The scene in front of the church was of total chaos and disarray, people were wounded, while others carried the bodies of loved ones.

CHAPTER TEN

Minister Grey, the reverends best friend looked up and saw the reverend and his family running towards the church and motioned for them to come to the back of the sanctuary. He met them and helped carry Grace into the building, after laying her down on the couch in her study. As they walked out of the study they went into the pastor's study were Minister Grey had pulled out the old scrolls and archives messages of yester years.

Minister Grey had written a timeline of unnatural events Grey asked him as the reverend out right what had he done, because, these events that was taking place could only be manifesting due to sins made by the reverend. Jon Jr. walked out of his father's study slamming the door behind him, he knew someone, someone on the pulpit had broken God's moral laws, what he did not know was that it was his father.

CHAPTER ELEVEN

The reverend stared at the board hearing his best friend asking him over and over what had he done? and all he could think about where her small round breast, tender red lips, her skin the color of rich caramel, jasmine scent and now she carried his seed. The reverend turned towards his friend, and just looking into his best friend's eyes he knew, he knew that his best friend, the reverend had taken his wife. Minister Grey walked over to him and punched him in the face breaking his nose, he turned over the desk, "Grey please forgive me."

the reverend shouted as Grey walked out of the study looking for his wife, when Olivia saw her husband come out of the study she knew he knew and ran out the church never to be seen are heard from again.

Jon Jr. saw the minister storm out his father's study, there was blood on his shirt, he ran into his father's office to find his father getting up off the floor. "Dad what happen? whats going on? Jon pleaded with his father, "It was I son," the reverend said with his eyes towards the ground unable to look his son in the eyes, all Jon could do was to stare at his father the man who walked upright before the lord and man now was slumped over and grieving for he had cost this devastation on the earth.

CHAPTER TWELVE

The Reverend stared out the window, shaking his head at the mess he had caused, there was screaming, fighting, blood shed all around him sexual immorality filling the streets, The 120 souls that were saved on that day were now being killed, stolen and destroyed by the Evil One, just as the blackbird spoken.

The only thing that could be done was to follow the dark shadow demons into the black forest of death and surrender his soul to save the decedents of the 120 and souls of their off springs.

CHAPTER THIRTEEN

Archangel Michael appeared before the reverend as he laid crying on the floor of his study. "Man of God, you must rise go and repent of your sins and lose your soul to the Evil One this is the only way to bring Our Father's salvation and peace upon the land once again." The reverend looked up in awe of the heavenliness standing before him and quickly shut his eyes and shivered into a ball, the angel of the Lord touched his shoulder saying be not afraid for He has sent me to you and we will fight side by side with you. He will be with you as you walk through the darkness and nothing will touch thee.

CHAPTER FOURTEEN

The reverend and a faithful few entered the forest of death repeating the 23rd Psalms

"The LORD is my shepherd; I shall not want. He maketh me to lie down in green pastures: he leadeth me beside the still waters. He restoreth my soul: he leadeth me in the paths of righteousness for his name's sake. Yea, though I walk through the valley of the shadow of death, I will fear no evil: for thou art with me; thy rod and thy staff they comfort me thou preparest a table before me in the presence of mine enemies: thou anointest my head with oil; my cup runneth over. Surely goodness and mercy shall follow me all the days of my life: and I will dwell in the house of the LORD forever."

CHAPTER FIFTEEN

As they crept through the forest of death, there were enemies on either side taunting and attempting to come at them through mental forces as well as physically., they could not be touched and when they did engage in hand to hand combat, Archangel Michael, and his army were there fighting with them side. The closer they got to the gates of hell they were met with strong heated winds, balls of fire shapeshifters and demon shadow's all shapes and sizes silently crying for help, for salvation for comfort and peace from the Evil One.

CHAPTER SIXTEEN

The smell of sulfur and burning brimstone overtook their senses. The reverend now turned to his wife because this was the end for him, he asked her for forgiveness as he told her about his adulterous affair with Grey's wife Grace loved her husband with all her heart, soul and body only Lord came before him. She was crying desperately seeking answers she knew not how to ask. Grace only knew how to be the good wife and did what any good wife would do in this situation, throw her arms around her husband and stand by her man.

The Evil One stood with a smirk on his face, not expecting Grace to forgive or stand by her man, he shook his head in disbelief saying "I didn't see that coming."

CHAPTER SEVENTEEN

The forest was dark and stale, the stench of sin was astounding, there standing at the "gates of hell was the Evil One and a numerous amount of what could only be called and or considered demon slaves "Man of God," the Evil One yelled out with a smirk across his wolf face as he licked his lips "What can I do you for?" he asked sarcastically as his demons laughed. "I come to save the souls you stole demon, by the grace of God!" the Evil One blurted out laughing "have you not forgotten man of God? you're the one who fell from His Grace just like me, so that makes us one. I guess you can say we're family."

Jonathan and the others stood side by side unwavering "I come to take back those souls you've stolen and make it right with God." Jonathan said loudly as the Evil One raised his eyebrows uncertain what to say to the man of God who stood strong before him. He stepped closer to Jonathan and the others with his goon squad behind him hissing like snakes with long sliver tongues and bodies of alligators. Once again the sky broke open as hail and lightning hit the ground between good and evil. Archangel Michael and his mighty army stood, armed with swords of the Lord, the Evil One took a step back. "Man of God you know what you must do? 'The Angel said, standing side by side with Jonathan and the other'. The battle began and the army of the Lord raised up breaking every chain.

CHAPTER EIGHTEEN

The Evil One shouted swinging his tail violently side by side using his claws to snap down trees although his goons ran and hid the army of the Lord stood tall and laugh, "You can laugh but I do win, man of God who couldn't keep his dick in his paints, the world will forever be smothered with sexual immorality because of your sins and my seed will walk upon the earth, rest assure on that day I'll be back, and, man of God the things I'm going to do to your descendants," he said as he began to rub his manhood hard until it became erect," I'm going to stick this into those tight innocent little boys and girls and ripped them apart, then I'm going to tear them limb from limb all this while they're." "Enough the angel roared as the ground began to pull the Evil One down, as if he was in quicksand. the reverend burst into flames as his wife jumped into the flames with him showing unconditional love and forgiveness they were sucked into the earth forever. Jon Jr. stood numb.

Part Two

"'Our Father in heaven, hallowed be your name,
[10] *your kingdom come, your will be done, on earth as it is in heaven.*
[11] *Give us today our daily bread.*
[12] *And forgive us our debts as we also have forgiven our debtors.*
[13] *And lead us not into temptation,[1] but deliver us from the evil one.*
Matthew 6:9-13, New International Version (NIV)

CHAPTER NINETEEN

A New Day . . .

The snow's beautiful as it falls silently to the ground, it takes my breath away with its gentleness and simplicity. I'm it sadden to have to walk through it and mess up its beauty. Everyone is so excited for this winter break, not me, I hate all breaks wish I could go to school and every after school program all year round, this way when I come home mom and Bob are stone and don't even realize I'm home.

CHAPTER TWENTY

"Ok guys, I want to wish everyone Merry Christmas and a Happy New Year."

Mr. Corey says to the class in his baritone smooth southern voice, he then preceded to walk around the class and hand out candy canes of different colors with stringy curly ribbon wrapped around them, with his bright smile says "My wife Faith is angelic." "Aye, I almost forgot and for the holidays, yes, don't look so surprise you have an assignment, a composition of Angelic it's meaning biblically and your own meaning of the word. Tamar I want to speak with you after class ok." Mr. Corey said quietly in my ear as he handed me my candy canes, I shook my head and turned towards the window watching the snow fall the silent and empty sound of the snow calms me.

CHAPTER TWENTY-ONE

The bell rang and everyone ran out the class as fast as possible excited to start winter break, if you ask me it's overrated, I wonder if my life was different would I feel like this? Would I hate going home? My mother has an awful crack habit and there's that entire my mother's a prostitute thing, for real I wouldn't know how to act in a different situation this life is all I know. Now that I've had this time to think about my current situation maybe my life's the norm and everybody else's life is messed up. "Hey you, what are you thinking about?" "I'm good Mr. Corey just looking at the snow." I said in my most convincing voice, I've learned to be a good actress, especially in front of Mr. Corey and his wife but he knew I was lying although he just smiled it was as if at that very moment he saw right through me in a good way not like Bob and the others.

CHAPTER TWENTY-TWO

"What are you doing for the holidays? "he asked as kindly and understanding as anyone who knew of my situation would," with a smile I said nothing much, hanging around the house "Tamar, that's what I want to talk to you about I Thin-;" "Stop right there, I don't want to hear it, I'm fine, yes my mom is who she is but she's my mom all we have is each other, it's not her fault she turned out the way she has, she was raped and got pregnant with me, so please stop and just pray for us, ok." I got up and quickly walked out the classroom before she could say anything else.

CHAPTER TWENTY-THREE

Mr. Corey seems so familiar; I've been in his class for the last two years perhaps that's what it is. His wife Faith is one of the youth pastors at the church and she is awesome, sometimes I wish she was my mother and he my dad.

They're like the coolest adults I know and she always smell like jasmine and he always has joke.

My mother and I use to attend the church but then she met Bob and we stopped going. Well, truth be told, I stay home to care for my mom somebody has to since she started using drugs again and prostituting. I knew he was bad news from the start but mom didn't listen to me are anyone else.

CHAPTER TWENTY-FOUR

I stand outside my building staring up at the sky breathing in the snow as it falls in my face making my skin feel tingly, and cold. It's amazing how just the feel of the snow on my face makes me feel fresh and clean. The snow is pure, innocent and clean. What does that make me?

CHAPTER TWENTY-FIVE

"This is an emergency interruption from the Governor of New York City." "As you know there has been a rush of rapes and killings over the last couple of weeks, sadly to say most of the victims have been between the ages of 6 and 12 years of age, please. I beg of you until we find this monster keep your children close to you."

CHAPTER TWENTY-SIX

"Honey, that's the third emergency interruption today." Faith said to her husband sitting down beside him on the couch as he studied the ancient document he held in his hands trembling. "Well babe, there's no doubt that my father made a mess and according to this document those children were direct descendants of the chosen few that went with my father to fight the Evil One." "There's absolutely no doubt in my mind that Tamar's mother is my first cousin." putting the document down he slide back with his eyes closed" Baby it's beginning, we have to go to the church I'll call the others" Jonathan said to Mercy kissing her on the forehead exiting the dining room repeating the Lord's Prayer.

"'Our Father in heaven, hallowed be your name,[10] your kingdom come, your will be done, on earth as it is in heaven.[11] Give us today our daily bread.[12] And forgive us our debts as we also have forgiven our debtors.[13] And lead us not into temptation,[j] but deliver us from the evil one. Matthew 6:9-13, New International Version (NIV)

CHAPTER TWENTY-SEVEN

Mom I'm hungry. This is the third night this week that I've gone to bed and haven't had nothing to eat. My name is Tamar and my mom is a drug addict and prostitute her boyfriend, her Pimp live with us. Some nights I sleep in abandoned cars outside of the projects where I live, because, it's safer than sleeping at home.

Lately my mom's been so cracked out that she's just not coherent to anything that's going on around her are around me. He looks at me and it makes me feel nasty, those eyes of his look me up and down. It feels like he's pulling my skin off every bone in my body while my blood vessel are being exposed to his touch.

He's a horrible man and I refused to let him see me afraid, I feel like If he sees my fear then he will swallow me whole And I will be no more.

It's the first day of Christmas break and I'm trying so hard to be quiet, not be seen but he knows I'm here. I can hear him walking past my room and to top it off he's turning my door knob knocking lightly on the door. I sit in my closet behind the little clothes I have, I look in my treasure box, I have a jar of peanut butter and jelly a whole and half loaf of bread and a gallon of water, near the window I have a bucket that I do my business in. Things are getting just a little critical nevertheless, I'll dump it when he leaves and take a shower.

CHAPTER TWENTY-EIGHT

I thought he left the house, it was so darn quiet, of course that was the clue quiet. I walk into the living room and there right in front of me was my mother having sex with what appeared to be several different men while Bob was having sex with several women it was so disgusting. When Bob and those men saw me they notice me \they proceeded to turn around and shake their disgusting dicks at me. I turned and ran as fast as I could, I didn't look back, there was a dark shadow chasing me. I could see it out the corner of my eye, I could feel the darkness breathing on my neck.

CHAPTER TWENTY-NINE

This morning I snuck into the living room to find my mother beaten to a pulp.

I helped her up off the floor into a shower, in which she smiles and tells me she loves me. Even though my mom's life isn't good, I remember when things were good just the two of us. We may not of had the best but what we had was ours and we had each other. Mom looks real old now even worn, I smiled back at her and underneath all that, I can still see her beauty.

As I get mom out the shower dry her off she seems so peaceful and content.

It's been weeks since she had on a pair of and for the first time in weeks she had on pajamas and her favorite red socks. Mom climbs bti the bed like a little girl and I tuck her in, give her kiss on her forehead. Mommy always tells me she's sorry and how much she loves me during these few quiet moments we share.

CHAPTER THIRTY

Bob stands outside the house off Merrick Blvd an 109th he watches the girl shelving the stoop as her mother dusts off the car in the driveway. The woman name Ruth looks up and sees her new friend standing there with a dozen roses, in excitement she covers her mouth and throws her arms around him, as he hugs her he smiles because he knows he's in hook line and sinker.

Ruth and Bob have been dating for six months now and she never brought anyone she has dated home to meet her daughter. Ruth sees the confused look in her daughter's eyes, she grabs Bob by the hand and walks over to her daughter.

Mary feels frighten unsure about this man a feeling of dread comes over her, "Mary this is my friend Bob," the hairs on Mary's neck stood straight up on her neck. As the man held his hand out to shake Mary's hand, she held her arms tightly on her sides smiling and saying hello walking off walked off into the family room where she shivered as if someone or something opened every window and door in the house.

CHAPTER THIRTY-0NE

Abolisher the Evil Ones leader of his army stared into the kitchen window at the evil young man kissing the very unsuspecting young women as passionately. He could sense as well as see the yearning desire, the need for him to be deep inside her. Well well well, "could this be him?" Abolisher asked his Sgt. "Look at him he's charming gentle, hell affectionate, if I wore panties I'll throw them at him and beg for him to take me." The others snickered, "let's go the master will be pleased."

CHAPTER THIRTY-TWO

Mary went directly to her room after dinner, several times during dinner she caught Bob looking at her, most uncomfortable. Once in her room she slide the lock on her door and fell asleep across her bed writing in her diary.

Ruth and Bob were making out on the couch she totally lost herself in this man.

She knew it was wrong, she heard the stories after all she herself was a direct descendent from the 120 and knew this was wrong, but she was lonely and this man made her feel alive, she thought as he slide his hands up her skirt and between her legs. Surely something so good can't be so wrong, Ruth opened her legs receiving his thick finger inside her the deeper he went the louder she moaned out for him to take her. Ruth's breath became short he lunged his tongue deep in her mouth as she accepted it with hunger her body slid back and forth to the rhythm of his fingers, until her hot moistness poured out of her only then did he drop to his knees parting her legs lickeing her click back and forth, harder and harder the wilder she became. Ruth was now begging for him to fuck her.

He carried her to her bedroom tore her clothes off threw her on the bed and rammed his manhood into her plunging deeper and deeper, she wrapped her legs around him. At that moment he knew he had her and soon he would have her daughter he thought to himself, as he began to cum he pulled out of her grabbed her by her hair and shoved his manhood into her mouth he knew once she tasted him he had her and she took all of it and it was done.

CHAPTER THIRTY-THREE

Jonathan and his wife sat on the first row of the church as the others began joining them in the sanctuary. The church suddenly began to breathe again you could almost hear the interior inhale and exhale breaths of life throughout the building.

The women began to remove the covering over the pulpit and throughout the sanctuary, one thing for certain everyone there had a place, a talent a gift for it was the only way for good to defeat the evil that was lurking and just the knowledge of knowing the evil one would indeed walk the earth again brought cold chills to the spins of all that where there.

CHAPTER THIRTY-FOUR

Jonathan stood at the head of the table with his wife standing by his side. the keepers of the scroll's dressed in white robes brought them to the table as the others along with Jon and his wife stood around the table.

The prophecy was written upon theses sacred scrolls, but could only be read after the minister of fire walked around the table anointing each one upon his head with oil whispering the lord's prayer:

Our Father in heaven, hallowed be your name

[10] your kingdom come, your will be done, on earth as it is in heaven.

[11] Give us today our daily bread.

[12] And forgive us our debts as we also have forgiven our debtors.

[13] And lead us not into temptation,[j] but deliver us from the evil one.

A storm began to rage on the sea of forgiveness which blew down trees and homes, some would say a tornado had fell upon the earth that night when indeed it was the evil that had been watching them grow and now knew that the battle would soon began.

CHAPTER THIRTY-FIVE

The Evil One looked out towards the earth searching high and low for His hos.

So many centuries had passed and not one person was that evil, the only common denominator in each century was sexual desire and lust for that of another." I can't believe I'm here stranded in my own kingdom! who he think he is anyway!! He can't do this. The world is full of lust and sexual immorality!!" The Evil One paced back and forth wildly as his servants coward folding upon the ground becoming one with the shadows. "There has to be one so evil that I can penetrate his body and become one with him, finding the descendants of the Reverend Jonathan Cooper and taking back what's rightfully mine!" He roared.

CHAPTER THIRTY-SIX

"Master we search the earth high low and I think we've come across one."

The Evil One slowly turned towards Abolisher raised his eyebrows and snarled, his face was shaped like a wolf his teeth were fangs his body was that of a man standing tall and strong on two hind legs with hooves as feet. There were scales all over his body and spikes from the back of his neck down to the tip of his tail which had an iron tip, that he swung from side to side ferociously. The Evil One stood seven feet tall a good two hundred and eighty pounds solid with three arms on each side of him as his hands were claws with long pointy razor sharp nails, like claws on an eagle.

CHAPTER THIRTY-SEVEN

As Abolisher spoke his voice was deep and firm. He stood at attention in front of his King, the servants in each room and corridor of hell fell fading into the ground like shadows, knowing that debauchery was going to take place in hell right here, right now.

The innocent souls cried trapped in the Evil Ones black iron treasure chest, knowing he would soon be coming for them. The time was finally here in which the Abolisher found the most evil man in all the earth, the one in whom the Evil One would be able to take possession of his body. This was the moment he'd been waiting for. As if on cue the servants went into the dark iron chambers where the Evil One's treasure chest where and grabbed out three of them placing them before their master in his torture room. The screams of the innocent souls became louder the more erect and hard the Evil One became, just knowing that he would be during the same thing on earth as he's doing now aroused him sexually in the worst way imaginable.

The Evil One couldn't stand the pressure anymore as he snatched open the first black box snatching out the first soul of an innocent. He began to brutally savagely plunging into her ripping into her, tearing her organs apart as she screamed for help. The more she screamed the more furious he became of his captivity in his hell, his servants now became aroused the onlookers and all the servants began sexing one another, it didn't matter animal or not the entire kingdom of hell was having an orgies in celebration of the Evil One's return to earth.

CHAPTER THIRTY-EIGHT

Each treasure chest held three virgins and as he finished with one chest he went on to the next chest, grabbing out the next virgin in which he rams into her harder than the last. Just the thought of those innocent waiting for him on earth aroused him even more as he plunged deeper into the next helpless soul before him harder and harder faster and faster he tears into the last virgin and reaches his climax. The Evil One roars and the earth shakes at it's thunderous sounds as hail begins to pour from the skies and the earth fades into darkness the Evil One steps into the 21st century with vengeance.

Part Three

"'Our Father in heaven, hallowed be your name
[10] your kingdom come, your will be done, on earth as it is in heaven.
[11] Give us today our daily bread.
[12] And forgive us our debts as we also have forgiven our debtors.
[13] And lead us not into temptation,[J] but deliver us from the evil one.
Matthew 6:9-13, New International Version (NIV)

CHAPTER THIRTY-NINE

Bob stepped in his tracks in front of his soon to be victim's house, he felt as if something or someone was noticing him. Bob smiled and slowly turned towards the street where Jonathan and the others were skillfully engaged in daily activities blending in with the others who lived unsuspectedly on the block.

CHAPTER FORTY

Bob disappeared in the blink of an eye to find himself-standing in hell before the throne of his father. "What the fuck is this?" Bob said with annoyance "What you will do, is bow before me the Evil One snarled standing to his feet, you are worthy enough to stand before me and live my son. Bob continued to stand straight and tall. The Evil One liked this "he certainly shows promise." the Evil One said to Abolisher as the other servant's scoured throughout the hall for some form of safety, after all no one disobeyed the master.

CHAPTER FORTY-ONE

The Evil One and Abolisher proceeded to tell Bob the story of how he came to be and how the future looked really good for him., he only had to accept and obey and all the pussy on the earth would belong to him. Bob accepted the challenge gracefully.

CHAPTER FORTY-TWO

"Where did he go?" Lille asked the others speaking into her ear piece, the others looked perplexed for Bob was just standing there. "The only explanation is that the Evil One knows he's his son, and, he brought him home for a visit." Mercy said reading the thermometer which showed signs of increase heat activity in the area, "It's getting dark let's go back to the church and come up with a plan."

Jonathan said as they began walking back to their trucks. "Station three how's Tamar and her mother?" "Jonathan there's has been no activity over here for days." Mark said shoving food in his mouth" Keep watching ok. Mary you ok?"

"I'm good sir although in this van with the human garbage disposer." She said looking at Mark as he winked his eye at her.

CHAPTER FORTY-THREE

Bob felt a sense of what he could only think happiness must feel like as he walked through the dark streets. Absolutely no demon from hell tried to attack him, but fall bowing down at his feet. Bob was exhilarated and horney trying to make his way to his latests victims and how he so desired to taste the girl as her mother watched, but, his manhood was so hard. Bob began rubbing on his manhood. He began to walk past old Ms. Loraine house and noticed she was peeping out the window.

The Evil One quickly entered his body and immediately put on that ever so charming smile of Bobis and ran up the porch steps as a concern citizen.

CHAPTER FORTY-FOUR

Ms. Loraine was so happy to see such a charming respectful young man looking out for the old in the neighborhood. She made them a cup of hot chocolate and took a fresh patch of sugar cookies out the oven, they sat in the living room talking about what was happening to the world as she had known it, such an attentive young man she thought to herself. He listened and the more she talked the angrier he became, she even paused to see if he had something to say, he just nodded for her to go on.

CHAPTER FORTY-FIVE

As Ms. Loraine sat in her living room waiting the young man to come back from putting the dishes in the sink, she hummed a little tune, she was so happy to have company. Bob walked back in the living room almost in a daze, she asked him if everything was ok but he said not a word, just walked straight to her. The closer he got to her she felt in her spirit that this was all wrong.

Ms. Loraine got out her seat to run for safety but he grabbed her by her neck threw her onto the floor ripping her clothes off. Once on the floor he got between her legs and ripped of her panties and rammed his hardness. The little old lady screamed as she faded in and out of darkness, only to be slapped back into her painful reality. He rammed her harder and harder as she lay like a ragdoll underneath him, she could only stare up at the ceiling praying for death to take her. She was bleeding through her mouth and blood ran from her nose and eyes as if tears were flowing throughout the insides of her frail now broken body.

CHAPTER FORTY-SIX

He could feel her insides tearing within her and this made the Ebil One even more excited he grunted and rammed as sweat popped off his face unto her face covered now in blood yet she was still alive barely breathing but faintly she was alive. When suddenly Bob felt a tap on his shoulders only then did he realize what he was doing, although he tried to stop he couldn't it was as if his body was being possessed. He looked over his shoulders and there standing behind him was his father.

CHAPTER FORTY-SEVEN

The Evil One managed to get underneath the women while his son was still ramming her, from the top. She could feel his scaly skin onto hers as she tried to scream for help, he then took his long finger nails and began to rub her arms as if caressing her for what was to come. Finally, he shoved his manhood into her from the back. Poor Ms. Loraine howled a terrible howl as the tip of his manhood, which was a metal tip penetrated her from the back as the iron made its way out the top of her head. The Evil One was pleased to see brain matter splattered throughout the living room causing both father and son to become even more aroused thus fucking her till her death.

CHAPTER FORTY-EIGHT

He's escalating rapidly Jonathan said kneeling next to the body. Faith broke out in prayer while the others tried to gather themselves and prepare for the task at hand.

We have to stop him before he gets to Tamar we only have 48 hours to send the Evil One and his son back to hell Faith explained to the others as if she was in a trance. "What are you talking about Faith? Jonathan asked curiously "is there something you would like to share?" Faith avoiding any eye contact with her husband and the others explained that the Evil One would get stronger the closer it got to Christmas, and, that not only had he come back to kill, steal and destroy he was going after the last living descendant of our Lord and Savior, Faith said softly.

CHAPTER FORTY-NINE

Mary went directly to her room after dinner, several times during dinner she caught Bob looking at her, most uncomfortable. Once in her room she slide the lock on her door and fell asleep across her bed writing in her diary.

Ruth and Bob were making out on the couch she totally lost herself in this man.

She knew it was wrong, she heard the stories after all she herself was a direct descendent from the 120 and knew this was wrong, but she was lonely and this man made her feel alive, she thought as he slide his hands up her skirt and between her legs. Surely something so good can't be so wrong, Ruth opened her legs receiving his thick finger inside her the deeper he went the louder she moaned out for him to take her. Ruth's breath became short he lunged his tongue deep in her mouth as she accepted it with hunger her body slid back and forth to the rhythm of his fingers, until her hot moistness poured out of her only then did he drop to his knees parting her legs lickeing her click back and forth, harder and harder the wilder she became. Ruth was now begging for him to fuck her.

He carried her to her bedroom tore her clothes off threw her on the bed and rammed his manhood into her plunging deeper and deeper, she wrapped her legs around him. At that moment he knew he had her and soon he would have her daughter he thought to himself, as he began to cum he pulled out of her grabbed her by her hair and shoved his manhood into her mouth he knew once she tasted him he had her and she took all of it and it was done.

CHAPTER FIFTY

Jonathan and his wife sat on the first row of the church as the others began joining them in the sanctuary. The church suddenly began to breathe again you could almost hear the interior inhale and exhale breaths of life throughout the building.

The women began to remove the covering over the pulpit and throughout the sanctuary, one thing for certain everyone there had a place, a talent a gift for it was the only way for good to defeat the evil that was lurking and just the knowledge of knowing the evil one would indeed walk the earth again brought cold chills to the spins of all that where there.

CHAPTER FIFTY-ONE

Jonathan stood at the head of the table with his wife standing by his side. the keepers of the scroll's dressed in white robes brought them to the table as the others along with Jon and his wife stood around the table.

The prophecy was written upon theses sacred scrolls, but could only be read after the minister of fire walked around the table anointing each one upon his head with oil whispering the lord's prayer:

Our Father in heaven, hallowed be your name,

[10] your kingdom come, your will be done, on earth as it is in heaven.

[11] Give us today our daily bread.

[12] And forgive us our debts as we also have forgiven our debtors.

[13] And lead us not into temptation,[j] but deliver us from the evil one.

A storm began to rage on the sea of forgiveness which blew down trees and homes, some would say a tornado had fell upon the earth that night when indeed it was the evil that had been watching them grow and now knew that the battle would soon began.

CHAPTER FIFTY-TWO

The Evil One looked out towards the earth searching high and low for His hos.

So many centuries had passed and not one person was that evil, the only common denominator in each century was sexual desire and lust for that of another." I can't believe I'm here stranded in my own kingdom! who he think he is anyway!! He can't do this. The world is full of lust and sexual immorality!!" The Evil One paced back and forth wildly as his servants coward folding upon the ground becoming one with the shadows. "There has to be one so evil that I can penetrate his body and become one with him, finding the descendants of the Reverend Jonathan Cooper and taking back what's rightfully mine!" He roared.

CHAPTER FIFTY-THREE

"Master we search the earth high low and I think we've come across one."

The Evil One slowly turned towards Abolisher raised his eyebrows and snarled, his face was shaped like a wolf his teeth were fangs his body was that of a man standing tall and strong on two hind legs with hooves as feet. There were scales all over his body and spikes from the back of his neck down to the tip of his tail which had an iron tip, that he swung from side to side ferociously. The Evil One stood seven feet tall a good two hundred and eighty pounds solid with three arms on each side of him as his hands were claws with long pointy razor sharp nails, like claws on an eagle.

CHAPTER FIFTY-FOUR

As Abolisher spoke his voice was deep and firm. He stood at attention in front of his King, the servants in each room and corridor of hell fell fading into the ground like shadows, knowing that debauchery was going to take place in hell right here, right now.

The innocent souls cried trapped in the Evil Ones black iron treasure chest, knowing he would soon be coming for them. The time was finally here in which the Abolisher found the most evil man in all the earth, the one in whom the Evil One would be able to take possession of his body. This was the moment he'd been waiting for. As if on cue the servants went into the dark iron chambers where the Evil One's treasure chest where and grabbed out three of them placing them before their master in his torture room. The screams of the innocent souls became louder the more erect and hard the Evil One became, just knowing that he would be during the same thing on earth as he's doing now aroused him sexually in the worst way imaginable.

The Evil One couldn't stand the pressure anymore as he snatched open the first black box snatching out the first soul of an innocent. He began to brutally savagely plunging into her ripping into her, tearing her organs apart as she screamed for help. The more she screamed the more furious he became of his captivity in his hell, his servants now became aroused the onlookers and all the servants began sexing one another, it didn't matter animal or not the entire kingdom of hell was having an orgies in celebration of the Evil One's return to earth.

CHAPTER FIFTY-FIVE

Each treasure chest held three virgins and as he finished with one chest he went on to the next chest, grabbing out the next virgin in which he rams into her harder than the last. Just the thought of those innocent waiting for him on earth aroused him even more as he plunged deeper into the next helpless soul before him harder and harder faster and faster he tears into the last virgin and reaches his climax. The Evil One roars and the earth hears it's thunderous sounds as hail begins to pour from the skies and the earth fades into darkness the Evil One steps into the 21st century with vengeance.

CHAPTER FIFTY-SIX

He's escalating rapidly Jonathan said kneeling next to the body. Faith broke out in prayer while the others tried to gather themselves and prepare for the task at hand.

We have to stop him before he gets to Tamar we only have 48 hours to send the Evil One and his son back to hell Faith explained to the others as if she was in a trance. "What are you talking about Faith? Jonathan asked curiously "is there something you would like to share?" Faith avoiding any eye contact with her husband and the others explained that the Evil One would get stronger the closer it got to Christmas, and, that not only had he come back to kill, steal and destroy he was going after the last living descendant of our Lord and Savior, Faith said softly.

Part Four

"'Our Father in heaven, hallowed be your name,
[10] your kingdom come, your will be done, on earth as it is in heaven.
[11] Give us today our daily bread.
[12] And forgive us our debts as we also have forgiven our debtors.
[13] And lead us not into temptation,[1] but deliver us from the evil one.
Matthew 6:9-13, New International Version (NIV)

CHAPTER FIFTY-SEVEN

The sky began to bleed as the rocks trembled and the earth once again openly received its unwanted guest. They preyed on the innocence in the land, their screams sent shivers up the bodies of the chosen few who fought alongside ArchAngel Michel to gain control over what would have been a lost world.

The demons that had enough of this life ran into the swords of the chosen few. Desperately seeking some form of redemption any form of peace away from the Evil One, while others fought until their death cursing our lord and savior as they screamed while the earth took them in for eternity.

CHAPTER FIFTY-EIGHT

The streets at dawn where as peaceful as a calm sea, not a demon insight, no screaming and no war, it's new day appeared before us as a ribbon of rainbows ever so gently stroked colors across its skies. Archangel Michael headed back to the spiritual realm to assist where he was needed as the others headed back to the solitude of the sanctuary. Praising and thanking God for yet a new day of his grace, His mercies and triumph over evil.

CHAPTER FIFTY-NINE

Jonathan paced the courtyard of the church several times before joining the others in the great room, he too was a man of vision as his father and those fathers before him. Jonathan stood on the banks of what use to be the river of forgiveness, suddenly he was taken back seeing things of yesterday through the eyes of his father. He began to remember his father being a true man of God one who worships the Lord and obeyed all God's commandments and stood steadfast on God's moral laws, his reputation was known throughout his congregation and surrounding communities.

CHAPTER SIXTY

The reverend was known as the visionary for he could see into the past, present and future and lately what he was envisioning about the future had him in complete despair a feeling he could not ignore. Jon saw through his father's eyes the river rising and the wind fiercely blowing as shivers ran up and down his body. The sky turned dark, bleeding into hail crying drops of blood throughout the pastures and roads, filling up the wells and streams with bloody water from the heavens above. Women and children began screaming running to the church for covering as the men huddled together attempting to figure out what was happening,

CHAPTER SIXTY-ONE

Through the eyes of his father, Jon could almost feel his father standing utterly still staring at what could only be a revelation in which his father was now seeing. Through the eyes of his father he saw a magnitude of sin, sin so great that the Evil One would walk the earth killing, stealing and destroy all innocence.

There would be wide spread incest, sexual immorality and drunkenness upon this the land that the Lord had given to his father's many years ago as he brought them out of darkness to this new land of plenty and at this very moment that land had turned into a well of blackness a well of black thick smoke which took his breath away.

CHAPTER SIXTY-TWO

Jon felt his breath leaving as he felt his father trying to catch his breath a black bird one with slick jet black feathers, yellow eyes and black claws stained with blood landed in front of him saying "Man of God on this Sunday one hundred and twenty souls will be baptized and cleansed in this the River of Forgiveness. These people will indeed repent of all their sins and be made whole by the blood of Jesus, know this man of God these one hundred and twenty souls that were cleansed and repented of their sins will be the first souls the Evil One will kill, steal and destroy, because, of the wickedness of your sins too come. Jon fell upon the ground into darkness after seeing this horror through the eyes of his father, only to wake up to his father crying kneeling prostrate to the ground crying "Holy Lord have mercy."

CHAPTER SIXTY-THREE

Jon saw through his father's eyes the death of the land that he knew now. A once so perfect land with beautiful rivers and streams began to dry and crumbled in despair, the once so beautiful valleys and greenery dries and also piled unto the dried earth. In a trance, his father looked across the blacken dried river into the forest of dark shadows. What Jon saw brought back remembrance of that night so long ago when his father and the others went into that very forest and fought with the Evil One with both hands and swords. Jon remembered his father turning to him before he burst into flames" son the Evil One is a trickster, what seems to be is not, he'll never fight on God's land, it may appear to be but it will not be, it will always be on earth as it is in the spiritual realm.

CHAPTER SIXTY-FOUR

Jonathan fell prostrate to the ground crying out unto the Lord with a sincere heart, his wife kneeling right next to him. The angel of the Lord stood before them smiling as bright as the sun, his skin was a golden copper that shined like bronze in the sun light, so bright they had to shield their eyes. "What do we do, Faith cried out bowing at the feet of the angel" I'm not worthy to be bowed down in front off, stand up and follow me." the angel said. "Know this you faithful of the Lord, He will always turn things around for the good of those who love him and He'll always use the least one, as His ram in the bush." Jonathan and Faith followed him into a garden which was filled with such beauty tears began to fall from their eyes and they began to praise God with gladness in their hearts, minds and soul.

CHAPTER SIXTY-FIVE

Bob was out of breath running from, well, he really wasn't sure why he was running, when he came to himself, he was covered in blood, smelling like flesh, when suddenly he heard the voice," well done son, you took out that old women like a champ." the Evil One laughed, as Bob shook his head, trying to clear the loud voice from his head, he began to remember what he done, and vomited, he felt sick, yes, sicker than normal and that's just a tad scary for he was a man with no boundaries, no morals but for the first time in his miserable existence he's feeling remorse. Bob stumbled to the ground at the sight that stood before him.

CHAPTER SIXTY-SIX

"Why son, you act like you've seen a monster." the Evil One said laughing, Bob covered his ears doe the voice of the monster standing in front of him was hard and loud. ""You freak, I don't know how you got inside me," Bob said getting up from the ground "but I work alone and I don't do old ladies man." the Evil One laughed saying "You do now son." "Yo stop calling me son, I'm not your son are anyones ass hole I'm a bastard made out of lust and all the evil in the world, now if you would excuse me I got women to do." Bob turned and walked away, not able to describe these funny feelings working in his body, unable to explain why he felt the need to keep that monster away from Ruth and Mary as he thought more about them he picked up his pace looking over his shoulder hoping not to be followed.

CHAPTER SIXTY-SEVEN

Jonathan and Faith joined the others and spoke of the angel, the garden and the mighty works the Lord was doing both on earth and in the spiritual realm, while the others stood watch outside Ruth and Martha's house for these where the two most important descendants by far, although the angels of the Lord stood side by side with them they did not see then; however ; they felt a sense of calm, some would even say peacefulness that suppresses all understanding.

CHAPTER SIXTY-EIGHT

Mary was in the kitchen helping her mother wash dishes, when suddenly she felt the need to go out on the front porch for some fresh air. It had been real quiet the last night or two, no screaming in the streets, no death, no bloodshed. What amazed Mary was that no evil came near their home for they were covered with the blood of the lamb, besides she thought to herself, "we are after all descendants of the chosen few," she just didn't know who.

CHAPTER SIXTY-NINE

The Evil One stood across the street from Ruth's house, peeping through the dried and brittle trees. He was staring at Mary salivating and rubbing his manhood, anticipating how he was going to rip and take her innocence and make her mother his whore for eternity. The hairs on his neck stood up, he couldn't see the angels but he knew they were somewhere around, he could smell them, the scent of roses made him want to puke "where's that son of mine at?" he whispered to himself.

CHAPTER SEVENTY

"There's someone knocking at the back door," Emmanuel whispered as he walked into the sanctuary. "Who would be knocking on the door?" Faith said inquisitively, I have no idea, Amina said as she looked at her husband, slowly the men walked towards the back door, each one with sword in hand. Jonathan could not believe his eyes when he looked out the stain glass window.

CHAPTER SEVENTY-ONE

Jonathan swung the door open and there standing in front of him was Bob, they stood and stared at one another while the others pointed their swords in Bob's direction. "I was under the impression that you christian folk was suppose to be much friendlier than this," he said looking towards the swords pointed at him.

Briana screamed" You're a murderer and a rapist, how dare you come into the house of the Lord." she yelled as the women pulled her back into the sanctuary.

"Ok, I admit, yes, I'm all those things and a lot more but I draw a line at someone taking over my mind and body to do freaky shit."

CHAPTER SEVENTY-TWO

Jonathan stepped aside as did the others so Bob could enter into the sanctuary, all eyes was on Bob as he walked into the conference room and took a seat. "I pictured this meeting different Bob said looking at Jonathan, the others were completely stunned, for in the light you could see just how much Jonathan and Bob looked alike. Jonathan offered Bob a seat and asked the others to give him a moment alone, reluctantly they exited the conference room." Listen I'm not here to make small talk, all I know is that when I looked up I was standing at the doors of the church. Listen, you need to know, he somehow gets in my body, and makes me do unspeakable things, things I wouldn't do on a bad day. He's going to try and use me to get to Ruth and Martha, he knows that Ruth is the direct descendant of Joseph and that Martha is the direct descendant of the Lord, he's going to punish them to get back at the Lord for what happened all those years ago. Listen I'm a bad man but this is even too much for me, so, big brother what are we going to do?

CHAPTER SEVENTY-THREE

The Evil One was getting disgusted, he needed to move in now, are he would bust, he saw a dog and possed it, slowly walking towards the porch where Mary stood, she saw the little dog and felt sorry for it, it was cold and hungry, she picked him up and brought him into the house. :Mary you know the rules, no animals."

Yea but he's cold and hungry, you could at least give this poor fella an exception to the rule, after all you've broken a few rules yourself ma." Ruth could do nothing but stare at her daughter knowing her words where true. "Ok just for tonight." The Evil One was ecstatic, he ran around hopping and humpping on their legs, "He's quite a little horney fella isn't he and they both laughed, the Evil One could do nothing for the body he chosen to possess was that of a poodle.

CHAPTER SEVENTY-FOUR

That night when Ruth and Mary was asleep, the Evil One was pacing back and forth, thinking of ways to torture his bastard son, for he could do nothing to ruth nor her daughter, it killed him that he couldn't taste her innocence and hear the horrible screams of a mother who could do nothing to help her child, then he heard it a drunk man stumbling pass the house, "he'll have to do." he snacthed the body up as if it was a toy, not noticing he was being watched he went back into the house reeking of alcohol and mildew, he would save the girl for last as her mother looked on, he opened Ruth's door slowly creeping towards the bed, trying to control himself, his manhood pulsing, he snatched the covers back and to his surprise there lying in the bed was Archangel Michael, he turned and ran to the girls room. Jonathan and the others were holding hands in prayer, he jumped out the window scouring into a place of safety, the Evil One was angry as hell for he had been deceived, he had been beaten on this night by good.

CHAPTER SEVENTY-FIVE

Everyone met back at the church, there were shouts of joy and praises to the almighty king for on this night they beat the Evil One at his own game, but, jonathan couldn't get his father's voice out of his head" He;s a trickster son,"

what's wrong Jonathan" William asked? "It seem to easy, something just doesn't feel right." Jonathan began looking around at the saints and realized Bob was missing, "O God he yelled, He's gone lets go everyone we have to get to Martha's house as soon as possible."

CHAPTER SEVENTY-SIX

As they got closer to Martha' and Tamar's house they could see the battle on the streets between the Lord's army and the Evil Ones, Jonathan and Archangel Michael broke away from the others and went around to the back of the building, where Jonathan climbed on Archangel Michael back and they flew to the 10th floor.

They looked in the window and there was Bob repeatedly beating Martha, she looked as if she was dead. Her lifeless body being thrown back and forth across the floor as Tamar tried to help. Bob sensed them as he cried for help, the Evil One laughed, Bob tried to fight the temptation that was within him but he continued to slap and kick Martha. Turning his sights unto Tamar, he put his hands around his neck, attempting to choke himself, when that didn't work he tried to jump out the window but the Evil One knew if he lost this vessel his plan would not work.

The Evil One knew once he penetrated Tamar that there would never be anymore good in the land it would be evil, evil would win and he would walk the earth for ever, as the Lord cried down upon the defeated world.

CHAPTER SEVENTY-SEVEN

The Evil One began ripping her clothes off as she fought him, Archangel Michael entered into the apartment in fury, his eyes was on fire, his sword burning like coal, Jonathan right behind him slaying the demons on every side, when the Evil One realized they had slayed all his demons he grabbed the girl and ran into the other room where Faith was waiting, her arms stretched wide repeating the Lord's Prayer as the earth shook violently, the Evil One had no choice but to let the girl go for the Lord was standing in the place and at the sight of the lord every knee bowed even the Evil One had no choice but to bow before the king, Bob fell down at the feet of the Lord, his body drained and mangled.

CHAPTER SEVENTY-EIGHT

The Lord was angry and all felt his wrath as the skies trembled and the earth shook. The angels bowed as the others fell prostrate to the ground, the Lord walked towards the Evil one and he cowered and backed against the wall, shaking trembling at the sound of the Lord. The Lord held his hand up and lightning came and hit the Evil One, he caught on fire and he and his demons was sentenced to the lake of fire for all eternity. Bob knew he could not be saved, he had did to much damage in the world, he didn't even ask for forgiveness he just jumped into the fiery lake and he too would burn for ever never to walk the earth again.

CHAPTER SEVENTY-NINE

When the smoke cleared and the earth was silenced in peace, the Lord walked though and waved his mighty right arm and peace, love and kindness became the earth. All sadness, pain and heartache was no more, the bodies of those taken by the Evil One was new and pure once again,.

The lesson the world learned from this horrible experience is that the Lord will use that very one that has hurt your body, mind and soul, He will use that very thing to turn what the enemy meant for evil around for your good. What a marvelous and wondrous God we serve.

The End

Printed in the United States
By Bookmasters